A Troll First-Start® Tall Tale

The Legend of Sleepy Hollow

by Patsy Jensen • illustrated by Rowan Barnes-Murphy

Troll Associates

The Ichabod Crane in this tall tale is a pretend person. But there may have been a real Ichabod Crane who lived on the banks of the Hudson River long ago.

A tall tale is an unusual story that has been exaggerated as it is retold over the years. Ichabod's tale shows how the power of imagination and storytelling can liven up our own everyday lives.

Library of Congress Cataloging-in-Publication Data

Jensen, Patricia.
  The legend of Sleepy Hollow / by Patricia A. Jensen; illustrated by Rowan S. Barnes-Murphy.
      p.   cm.(A Troll first-start tall tale)
  Based on the story by Washington Irving.
  Summary: A superstitious schoolmaster, in love with a wealthy farmer's daughter, has a terrifying encounter with a headless horseman.
  ISBN 0-8167-3168-3 (library)   ISBN 0-8167-3169-1 (pbk.)
  [1. Ghosts—Fiction.   2. New York (State)—Fiction.]   I. Irving, Washington, 1783-1959.   Legend of Sleepy Hollow.   II. Barnes-Murphy, Rowan, ill.   III. Title.   IV. Series.
PZ7.J438Le   1994
[E]—dc20   93-24803

Printed in the United States of America.
10 9 8 7 6 5 4 3 2 1

Ichabod Crane was the schoolmaster in a quiet little village called Sleepy Hollow.

Sleepy Hollow lay in a peaceful valley near the Hudson River. Nothing much ever happened in Sleepy Hollow. Every day was just like the one before it.

Ichabod boarded with different families in Sleepy Hollow. He lived a week at one house, then a week at another.

At every house, Ichabod would hear the story of a mysterious rider who roamed the woods at night on a fast, dark horse.

This story scared Ichabod. Why?

Because the rider had no head!

The story said that this rider had been a soldier in the Revolutionary War. His head had been shot off by a cannonball, and his body was buried in a church graveyard. At night his ghost rode through the woods, looking for his missing head.

Every time Ichabod heard the story, he
would lay awake trembling all night long.
But the people of Sleepy Hollow loved to tell
the tale of the Headless Horseman.

There was one place where Ichabod did not mind hearing the story. That was at the Van Tassel farm, the home of the richest family in Sleepy Hollow.

Ichabod was in love with Katrina Van Tassel, a beautiful young woman who took singing lessons from him. Whenever the tale of the Headless Horseman was told at the Van Tassel farm, Ichabod was too busy gazing at Katrina to listen.

Ichabod dreamed about all the money
he would have if he and Katrina got married.

The only problem was that Katrina had another beau. His name was Brom Bones. And he was as handsome and dashing as Ichabod was homely and dull.

But Katrina was fond of Ichabod
because he was very smart and had read
many books. As far as she knew, Brom Bones
had never read a single book.

Brom realized that Katrina might choose Ichabod, so he set out to drive Ichabod away. The first thing he did was to stuff up the chimney at the house where Ichabod was giving singing lessons. All the young ladies and Ichabod had to run outside to get away from the smoke.

The next thing Brom did was to spill all the inkwells and turn over all the desks at the school.

"You should fight Brom and put a stop to his tricks," Katrina told Ichabod.

But Ichabod was too frightened of Brom to fight him.

"He's just having a little fun," Ichabod said.

One day after school, a servant boy rode
up to the schoolhouse. Ichabod was invited
to a party at the Van Tassel house that
evening.

Ichabod was very excited. He rushed home to get ready for the party. After he washed up, Ichabod put on his finest suit.

Ichabod borrowed an old horse and headed through the woods as the sun was setting. Even though his suit was a bit tattered and worn, Ichabod felt dashing and handsome.

"Tonight I shall propose to Katrina," he decided.

At the Van Tassel farm, the party had
already begun. Ichabod had never seen such
fine clothes and wonderful food. He danced
with Katrina and had a wonderful time—until
Brom Bones showed up and began to tell a
scary story.

"I met the Headless Horseman last night," said Brom.

A crowd gathered around him.

"He tried to race me," Brom continued. "We were riding along neck and neck until we came to the church bridge."

Everyone gathered closer to hear Brom. "Then what happened?" someone asked.

"When we got to the bridge," Brom said, "the Headless Horseman vanished in a flash of fire!"

Ichabod felt a chill creeping along his skinny arms. His hair rose on his neck as he thought of the long, lonely ride home through the dark woods.

After the party was over, Ichabod spoke
to Katrina. No one heard what they said.
But Ichabod looked very sad when he left.
He leaped onto his horse and began racing
through the woods as quickly as possible.
The story of the Headless Horseman was on
his mind.

Ichabod's heart was pounding. Finally he saw the brook ahead.

"It's not far now," Ichabod told himself. "Giddy-up!" he shouted to his horse.

Suddenly the horse stopped in its tracks. Ichabod looked up and saw a dark figure in the moonlight.

"Who's there?" he called, terrified. "Who's there?"

The figure came closer and closer. Ichabod could now see that it was a headless rider. And he was carrying his own head in front of him!

Ichabod screamed and dug his heels into his horse. With a great leap, the horse began racing toward the church bridge.

"If only I can make it to the bridge," Ichabod thought. "Then the rider will vanish into flames."

But when Ichabod reached the bridge, the rider was right behind him. He didn't vanish in a flash of fire. Then, before Ichabod had a moment to think, the rider threw his head at the terrified schoolmaster.

The next morning Ichabod's hat was found lying on the church bridge—next to a smashed pumpkin.

But Ichabod Crane was never heard from or seen again. Some people say that the Headless Horseman caught him to borrow his head. They say you can sometimes hear a strange moaning sound by the churchyard.

But if you ask Brom Bones what happened to Ichabod Crane, the only answer you'll get is a smile.